This Journal

BELONGS TO

_____

_____

Dedication

This Restaurant Review Journal is dedicated to all the people out there who love to track their Restaurant Reviews and document their findings in the process.

You are my inspiration for producing books and I'm honored to be a part of keeping all of your Restaurant notes, and records organized.

This journal notebook will help you record your details about tracking your dining out experiences.

Thoughtfully put together with these sections to record: Restaurant Name, Party Members, Service, Beverage Service, Cleanliness, Overall Review, Impressions, Mileage, & Compensation Received.

How to Use this Book

The purpose of this book is to keep all of your Restaurant Review notes all in one place. It will help keep you organized.

This Restaurant Journal Book will allow you to accurately document every detail about all of your dining out experiences. It's a great way to chart your course through Restaurant Reviewing.

Here are examples of the prompts for you to fill in and write about your experience in this book:

1. Restaurant Name- Restaurant Name, Date of Visit, Time of Reservation, Server Name, Manager on Duty

2. Party Members - Names, Meals Ordered, Quality, Price

3. Service - Warm Welcome?, Attentiveness & Pace of Service, Gave Good Recommendations?, Accuracy of Service.

4. Beverage Service - Good Recommendations?, Experience Details?

5. Cleanliness - Restaurant Cleanliness, Restroom Cleanliness

6. Overall Review & Impressions - Would You Recommend?, Opportunities for Improvement.

7. Mileage, Compensation, Received - Blank Lined to Write Your Number

Restaurant _____ Date of visit _____ Time _____

Server name _____ Manager on duty _____

Party member	Meal ordered	Quality	Price
		Total	

Server

Warm welcome? _____

Attentiveness and pace of service _____

Gave good recommendations? _____

Accuracy of service _____

Beverage Service

Good recommendations? _____ Checked ID? _____

Experience? _____ Quality of drinks _____

Restaurant

Restaurant cleanliness _____

Restroom cleanliness _____

Overall Impressions

Would you recommend this restaurant? _____

Opportunities for improvement _____

Mileage _____ Compensation _____ Received _____

Restaurant _____   Date of visit _____   Time _____

Server name _____   Manager on duty _____

Party member	Meal ordered	Quality	Price
		Total	

Server

Warm welcome? _____

Attentiveness and pace of service _____

Gave good recommendations? _____

Accuracy of service _____

Beverage Service

Good recommendations? _____   Checked ID? _____

Experience? _____   Quality of drinks _____

Restaurant

Restaurant cleanliness _____

Restroom cleanliness _____

Overall Impressions

Would you recommend this restaurant? _____

Opportunities for improvement _____

Mileage _____   Compensation _____   Received _____

Restaurant _____ Date of visit _____ Time _____

Server name _____ Manager on duty _____

Party member	Meal ordered	Quality	Price
		Total	

Server

Warm welcome? _____

Attentiveness and pace of service _____

Gave good recommendations? _____

Accuracy of service _____

Beverage Service

Good recommendations? _____ Checked ID? _____

Experience? _____ Quality of drinks _____

Restaurant

Restaurant cleanliness _____

Restroom cleanliness _____

Overall Impressions

Would you recommend this restaurant? _____

Opportunities for improvement _____

Mileage _____ Compensation _____ Received _____

Restaurant _____ Date of visit _____ Time _____

Server name _____ Manager on duty _____

Party member	Meal ordered	Quality	Price
		Total	

Server

Warm welcome? _____

Attentiveness and pace of service _____

Gave good recommendations? _____

Accuracy of service _____

Beverage Service

Good recommendations? _____ Checked ID? _____

Experience? _____ Quality of drinks _____

Restaurant

Restaurant cleanliness _____

Restroom cleanliness _____

Overall Impressions

Would you recommend this restaurant? _____

Opportunities for improvement _____

Mileage _____ Compensation _____ Received _____

Restaurant _____ Date of visit _____ Time _____

Server name _____ Manager on duty _____

Party member	Meal ordered	Quality	Price
		Total	

Server

Warm welcome? _____

Attentiveness and pace of service _____

Gave good recommendations? _____

Accuracy of service _____

Beverage Service

Good recommendations? _____   Checked ID? _____

Experience? _____   Quality of drinks _____

Restaurant

Restaurant cleanliness _____

Restroom cleanliness _____

Overall Impressions

Would you recommend this restaurant? _____

Opportunities for improvement _____

Mileage _____   Compensation _____   Received _____

Restaurant _____ Date of visit _____ Time _____

Server name _____ Manager on duty _____

Party member	Meal ordered	Quality	Price
	Total		

--- **Server** ---

Warm welcome? _____

Attentiveness and pace of service _____

Gave good recommendations? _____

Accuracy of service _____

--- **Beverage Service** ---

Good recommendations? _____ Checked ID? _____

Experience? _____ Quality of drinks _____

--- **Restaurant** ---

Restaurant cleanliness _____

Restroom cleanliness _____

--- **Overall Impressions** ---

Would you recommend this restaurant? _____

Opportunities for improvement _____

Mileage _____ Compensation _____ Received _____

Restaurant _____ Date of visit _____ Time _____

Server name _____ Manager on duty _____

Party member	Meal ordered	Quality	Price
		Total	

Server

Warm welcome? _____

Attentiveness and pace of service _____

Gave good recommendations? _____

Accuracy of service _____

Beverage Service

Good recommendations? _____ Checked ID? _____

Experience? _____ Quality of drinks _____

Restaurant

Restaurant cleanliness _____

Restroom cleanliness _____

Overall Impressions

Would you recommend this restaurant? _____

Opportunities for improvement _____

Mileage _____ Compensation _____ Received _____

Restaurant _____ Date of visit _____ Time _____

Server name _____ Manager on duty _____

Party member	Meal ordered	Quality	Price
		Total	

Server

Warm welcome? _____

Attentiveness and pace of service _____

Gave good recommendations? _____

Accuracy of service _____

Beverage Service

Good recommendations? _____ Checked ID? _____

Experience? _____ Quality of drinks _____

Restaurant

Restaurant cleanliness _____

Restroom cleanliness _____

Overall Impressions

Would you recommend this restaurant? _____

Opportunities for improvement _____

Mileage _____ Compensation _____ Received _____

Restaurant _____ Date of visit _____ Time _____

Server name _____ Manager on duty _____

Party member	Meal ordered	Quality	Price
		Total	

Server

Warm welcome? _____

Attentiveness and pace of service _____

Gave good recommendations? _____

Accuracy of service _____

Beverage Service

Good recommendations? _____ Checked ID? _____

Experience? _____ Quality of drinks _____

Restaurant

Restaurant cleanliness _____

Restroom cleanliness _____

Overall Impressions

Would you recommend this restaurant? _____

Opportunities for improvement _____

Mileage _____ Compensation _____ Received _____

Restatant _____   Date of visit _____   Time _____

Server name _____   Manager on duty _____

Party member	Meal ordered	Quality	Price
		Total	

Server

Warm welcome? _____

Attentiveness and pace of service _____

Gave good recommendations? _____

Accuracy of service _____

Beverage Service

Good recommendations? _____   Checked ID? _____

Experience? _____   Quality of drinks _____

Restaurant

Restaurant cleanliness _____

Restroom cleanliness _____

Overall Impressions

Would you recommend this restaurant? _____

Opportunities for improvement _____

Mileage _____   Compensation _____   Received _____

Restaurant _____ Date of visit _____ Time _____

Server name _____ Manager on duty _____

Party member	Meal ordered	Quality	Price
		Total	

Server

Warm welcome? _____

Attentiveness and pace of service _____

Gave good recommendations? _____

Accuracy of service _____

Beverage Service

Good recommendations? _____ Checked ID? _____

Experience? _____ Quality of drinks _____

Restaurant

Restaurant cleanliness _____

Restroom cleanliness _____

Overall Impressions

Would you recommend this restaurant? _____

Opportunities for improvement _____

Mileage _____ Compensation _____ Received _____

Restaurant _____ Date of visit _____ Time _____

Server name _____ Manager on duty _____

Party member	Meal ordered	Quality	Price
	Total		

Server

Warm welcome? _____

Attentiveness and pace of service _____

Gave good recommendations? _____

Accuracy of service _____

Beverage Service

Good recommendations? _____   Checked ID? _____

Experience? _____   Quality of drinks _____

Restaurant

Restaurant cleanliness _____

Restroom cleanliness _____

Overall Impressions

Would you recommend this restaurant? _____

Opportunities for improvement _____

Mileage _____   Compensation _____   Received _____

Restaurant _____ Date of visit _____ Time _____

Server name _____ Manager on duty _____

Party member	Meal ordered	Quality	Price
		Total	

Server

Warm welcome? _____

Attentiveness and pace of service _____

Gave good recommendations? _____

Accuracy of service _____

Beverage Service

Good recommendations? _____   Checked ID? _____

Experience? _____   Quality of drinks _____

Restaurant

Restaurant cleanliness _____

Restroom cleanliness _____

Overall Impressions

Would you recommend this restaurant? _____

Opportunities for improvement _____

Mileage _____   Compensation _____   Received _____

Restaurant _____ Date of visit _____ Time _____

Server name _____ Manager on duty _____

Party member	Meal ordered	Quality	Price
		Total	

Server

Warm welcome? _____

Attentiveness and pace of service _____

Gave good recommendations? _____

Accuracy of service _____

Beverage Service

Good recommendations? _____ Checked ID? _____

Experience? _____ Quality of drinks _____

Restaurant

Restaurant cleanliness _____

Restroom cleanliness _____

Overall Impressions

Would you recommend this restaurant? _____

Opportunities for improvement _____

Mileage _____ Compensation _____ Received _____

Restaurant _____ Date of visit _____ Time _____

Server name _____ Manager on duty _____

Party member	Meal ordered	Quality	Price
		Total	

Server

Warm welcome? _____

Attentiveness and pace of service _____

Gave good recommendations? _____

Accuracy of service _____

Beverage Service

Good recommendations? _____ Checked ID? _____

Experience? _____ Quality of drinks _____

Restaurant

Restaurant cleanliness _____

Restroom cleanliness _____

Overall Impressions

Would you recommend this restaurant? _____

Opportunities for improvement _____

Mileage _____ Compensation _____ Received _____

Restaurant _____ Date of visit _____ Time _____

Server name _____ Manager on duty _____

Party member	Meal ordered	Quality	Price
		Total	

Server

Warm welcome? _____

Attentiveness and pace of service _____

Gave good recommendations? _____

Accuracy of service _____

Beverage Service

Good recommendations? _____ Checked ID? _____

Experience? _____ Quality of drinks _____

Restaurant

Restaurant cleanliness _____

Restroom cleanliness _____

Overall Impressions

Would you recommend this restaurant? _____

Opportunities for improvement _____

Mileage _____ Compensation _____ Received _____

Restaurant		Date of visit	Time

Server name _____   Manager on duty _____

Party member	Meal ordered	Quality	Price
		Total	

Server

Warm welcome? _____

Attentiveness and pace of service _____

Gave good recommendations? _____

Accuracy of service _____

Beverage Service

Good recommendations? _____   Checked ID? _____

Experience? _____   Quality of drinks _____

Restaurant

Restaurant cleanliness _____

Restroom cleanliness _____

Overall Impressions

Would you recommend this restaurant? _____

Opportunities for improvement _____

Mileage _____   Compensation _____   Received _____

Restaurant _____ Date of visit _____ Time _____

Server name _____ Manager on duty _____

Party member	Meal ordered	Quality	Price
		Total	

┌─ **Server** ─────────────────────────────────┐

Warm welcome? _____

Attentiveness and pace of service _____

Gave good recommendations? _____

Accuracy of service _____

└──┘

┌─ **Beverage Service** ────────────────────────┐

Good recommendations? _____ Checked ID? _____

Experience? _____ Quality of drinks _____

└──┘

┌─ **Restaurant** ──────────────────────────────┐

Restaurant cleanliness _____

Restroom cleanliness _____

└──┘

┌─ **Overall Impressions** ─────────────────────┐

Would you recommend this restaurant? _____

Opportunities for improvement _____

└──┘

Mileage _____ Compensation _____ Received _____

Restaurant _____ Date of visit _____ Time _____

Server name _____ Manager on duty _____

Party member	Meal ordered	Quality	Price
		Total	

┌─ **Server** ─────────────────────────────────┐

Warm welcome? _____

Attentiveness and pace of service _____

Gave good recommendations? _____

Accuracy of service _____

└──┘

┌─ **Beverage Service** ───────────────────────┐

Good recommendations? _____ Checked ID? _____

Experience? _____ Quality of drinks _____

└──┘

┌─ **Restaurant** ─────────────────────────────┐

Restaurant cleanliness _____

Restroom cleanliness _____

└──┘

┌─ **Overall Impressions** ────────────────────┐

Would you recommend this restaurant? _____

Opportunities for improvement _____

└──┘

Mileage _____ Compensation _____ Received _____

Restaurant _____ Date of visit _____ Time _____

Server name _____ Manager on duty _____

Party member	Meal ordered	Quality	Price
		Total	

Server

Warm welcome? _____

Attentiveness and pace of service _____

Gave good recommendations? _____

Accuracy of service _____

Beverage Service

Good recommendations? _____   Checked ID? _____

Experience? _____   Quality of drinks _____

Restaurant

Restaurant cleanliness _____

Restroom cleanliness _____

Overall Impressions

Would you recommend this restaurant? _____

Opportunities for improvement _____

Mileage _____   Compensation _____   Received _____

Restaurant _____   Date of visit _____   Time _____

Server name _____   Manager on duty _____

Party member	Meal ordered	Quality	Price
		Total	

┌─── **Server** ────────────────────────────────┐

Warm welcome? _____

Attentiveness and pace of service _____

Gave good recommendations? _____

Accuracy of service _____

└──┘

┌─── **Beverage Service** ──────────────────────┐

Good recommendations? _____   Checked ID? _____

Experience? _____   Quality of drinks _____

└──┘

┌─── **Restaurant** ────────────────────────────┐

Restaurant cleanliness _____

Restroom cleanliness _____

└──┘

┌─── **Overall Impressions** ───────────────────┐

Would you recommend this restaurant? _____

Opportunities for improvement _____

└──┘

Mileage _____   Compensation _____   Received _____

Restaurant _____ Date of visit _____ Time _____

Server name _____ Manager on duty _____

Party member	Meal ordered	Quality	Price
	Total		

Server

Warm welcome? _____

Attentiveness and pace of service _____

Gave good recommendations? _____

Accuracy of service _____

Beverage Service

Good recommendations? _____   Checked ID? _____

Experience? _____   Quality of drinks _____

Restaurant

Restaurant cleanliness _____

Restroom cleanliness _____

Overall Impressions

Would you recommend this restaurant? _____

Opportunities for improvement _____

Mileage _____   Compensation _____   Received _____

Restaurant _____ Date of visit _____ Time _____

Server name _____ Manager on duty _____

Party member	Meal ordered	Quality	Price
		Total	

Server

Warm welcome? _____

Attentiveness and pace of service _____

Gave good recommendations? _____

Accuracy of service _____

Beverage Service

Good recommendations? _____ Checked ID? _____

Experience? _____ Quality of drinks _____

Restaurant

Restaurant cleanliness _____

Restroom cleanliness _____

Overall Impressions

Would you recommend this restaurant? _____

Opportunities for improvement _____

Mileage _____ Compensation _____ Received _____

Restaurant _____ Date of visit _____ Time _____

Server name _____ Manager on duty _____

Party member	Meal ordered	Quality	Price
		Total	

Server

Warm welcome? _____

Attentiveness and pace of service _____

Gave good recommendations? _____

Accuracy of service _____

Beverage Service

Good recommendations? _____ Checked ID? _____

Experience? _____ Quality of drinks _____

Restaurant

Restaurant cleanliness _____

Restroom cleanliness _____

Overall Impressions

Would you recommend this restaurant? _____

Opportunities for improvement _____

Mileage _____ Compensation _____ Received _____

Restaurant _____ Date of visit _____ Time _____

Server name _____ Manager on duty _____

Party member	Meal ordered	Quality	Price
		Total	

Server

Warm welcome? _____

Attentiveness and pace of service _____

Gave good recommendations? _____

Accuracy of service _____

Beverage Service

Good recommendations? _____ Checked ID? _____

Experience? _____ Quality of drinks _____

Restaurant

Restaurant cleanliness _____

Restroom cleanliness _____

Overall Impressions

Would you recommend this restaurant? _____

Opportunities for improvement _____

Mileage _____ Compensation _____ Received _____

Restaurant _____ Date of visit _____ Time _____

Server name _____ Manager on duty _____

Party member	Meal ordered	Quality	Price
		Total	

Server

Warm welcome? _____

Attentiveness and pace of service _____

Gave good recommendations? _____

Accuracy of service _____

Beverage Service

Good recommendations? _____ Checked ID? _____

Experience? _____ Quality of drinks _____

Restaurant

Restaurant cleanliness _____

Restroom cleanliness _____

Overall Impressions

Would you recommend this restaurant? _____

Opportunities for improvement _____

Mileage _____ Compensation _____ Received _____

Restaurant _____ Date of visit _____ Time _____

Server name _____ Manager on duty _____

Party member	Meal ordered	Quality	Price
		Total	

┌─ **Server** ─────────────────────────────────┐

Warm welcome? _____

Attentiveness and pace of service _____

Gave good recommendations? _____

Accuracy of service _____

└──┘

┌─ **Beverage Service** ───────────────────────┐

Good recommendations? _____ Checked ID? _____

Experience? _____ Quality of drinks _____

└──┘

┌─ **Restaurant** ─────────────────────────────┐

Restaurant cleanliness _____

Restroom cleanliness _____

└──┘

┌─ **Overall Impressions** ────────────────────┐

Would you recommend this restaurant? _____

Opportunities for improvement _____

└──┘

Mileage _____ Compensation _____ Received _____

Restaurant _____ Date of visit _____ Time _____

Server name _____ Manager on duty _____

Party member	Meal ordered	Quality	Price
		Total	

Server

Warm welcome? _____

Attentiveness and pace of service _____

Gave good recommendations? _____

Accuracy of service _____

Beverage Service

Good recommendations? _____ Checked ID? _____

Experience? _____ Quality of drinks _____

Restaurant

Restaurant cleanliness _____

Restroom cleanliness _____

Overall Impressions

Would you recommend this restaurant? _____

Opportunities for improvement _____

Mileage _____ Compensation _____ Received _____

Restaurant _____ Date of visit _____ Time _____

Server name _____ Manager on duty _____

Party member	Meal ordered	Quality	Price
		Total	

Server

Warm welcome? _____

Attentiveness and pace of service _____

Gave good recommendations? _____

Accuracy of service _____

Beverage Service

Good recommendations? _____   Checked ID? _____

Experience? _____   Quality of drinks _____

Restaurant

Restaurant cleanliness _____

Restroom cleanliness _____

Overall Impressions

Would you recommend this restaurant? _____

Opportunities for improvement _____

Mileage _____   Compensation _____   Received _____

Restaurant _____ Date of visit _____ Time _____

Server name _____ Manager on duty _____

Party member	Meal ordered	Quality	Price
		Total	

┌─ **Server** ─────────────────────────────────┐

Warm welcome? _____

Attentiveness and pace of service _____

Gave good recommendations? _____

Accuracy of service _____

└──┘

┌─ **Beverage Service** ───────────────────────┐

Good recommendations? _____ Checked ID? _____

Experience? _____ Quality of drinks _____

└──┘

┌─ **Restaurant** ─────────────────────────────┐

Restaurant cleanliness _____

Restroom cleanliness _____

└──┘

┌─ **Overall Impressions** ────────────────────┐

Would you recommend this restaurant? _____

Opportunities for improvement _____

└──┘

Mileage _____ Compensation _____ Received _____

Restaurant _____ Date of visit _____ Time _____

Server name _____ Manager on duty _____

Party member	Meal ordered	Quality	Price
		Total	

Server

Warm welcome? _____

Attentiveness and pace of service _____

Gave good recommendations? _____

Accuracy of service _____

Beverage Service

Good recommendations? _____ Checked ID? _____

Experience? _____ Quality of drinks _____

Restaurant

Restaurant cleanliness _____

Restroom cleanliness _____

Overall Impressions

Would you recommend this restaurant? _____

Opportunities for improvement _____

Mileage _____ Compensation _____ Received _____

Restaurant _____ Date of visit _____ Time _____

Server name _____ Manager on duty _____

Party member	Meal ordered	Quality	Price
		Total	

Server

Warm welcome? _____

Attentiveness and pace of service _____

Gave good recommendations? _____

Accuracy of service _____

Beverage Service

Good recommendations? _____ Checked ID? _____

Experience? _____ Quality of drinks _____

Restaurant

Restaurant cleanliness _____

Restroom cleanliness _____

Overall Impressions

Would you recommend this restaurant? _____

Opportunities for improvement _____

Mileage _____ Compensation _____ Received _____

Restaurant _____ Date of visit _____ Time _____

Server name _____ Manager on duty _____

Party member	Meal ordered	Quality	Price
		Total	

┌─ **Server** ─────────────────────────┐

Warm welcome? _____

Attentiveness and pace of service _____

Gave good recommendations? _____

Accuracy of service _____

└──────────────────────────────────────┘

┌─ **Beverage Service** ────────────────┐

Good recommendations? _____ Checked ID? _____

Experience? _____ Quality of drinks _____

└──────────────────────────────────────┘

┌─ **Restaurant** ──────────────────────┐

Restaurant cleanliness _____

Restroom cleanliness _____

└──────────────────────────────────────┘

┌─ **Overall Impressions** ─────────────┐

Would you recommend this restaurant? _____

Opportunities for improvement _____

└──────────────────────────────────────┘

Mileage _____ Compensation _____ Received _____

Restaurant _____ Date of visit _____ Time _____

Server name _____ Manager on duty _____

Party member	Meal ordered	Quality	Price
	Total		

Server

Warm welcome? _____

Attentiveness and pace of service _____

Gave good recommendations? _____

Accuracy of service _____

Beverage Service

Good recommendations? _____ Checked ID? _____

Experience? _____ Quality of drinks _____

Restaurant

Restaurant cleanliness _____

Restroom cleanliness _____

Overall Impressions

Would you recommend this restaurant? _____

Opportunities for improvement _____

Mileage _____ Compensation _____ Received _____

| Restaurant | | Date of visit | | Time | |

Restaurant _____   Date of visit _____   Time _____

Server name _____   Manager on duty _____

Party member	Meal ordered	Quality	Price
		Total	

Server

Warm welcome? _____

Attentiveness and pace of service _____

Gave good recommendations? _____

Accuracy of service _____

Beverage Service

Good recommendations? _____   Checked ID? _____

Experience? _____   Quality of drinks _____

Restaurant

Restaurant cleanliness _____

Restroom cleanliness _____

Overall Impressions

Would you recommend this restaurant? _____

Opportunities for improvement _____

Mileage _____   Compensation _____   Received _____

Restaurant _____ Date of visit _____ Time _____

Server name _____ Manager on duty _____

Party member	Meal ordered	Quality	Price
		Total	

--- **Server** ---

Warm welcome? _____

Attentiveness and pace of service _____

Gave good recommendations? _____

Accuracy of service _____

--- **Beverage Service** ---

Good recommendations? _____ Checked ID? _____

Experience? _____ Quality of drinks _____

--- **Restaurant** ---

Restaurant cleanliness _____

Restroom cleanliness _____

--- **Overall Impressions** ---

Would you recommend this restaurant? _____

Opportunities for improvement _____

Mileage _____ Compensation _____ Received _____

Restaurant _____   Date of visit _____   Time _____

Server name _____   Manager on duty _____

Party member	Meal ordered	Quality	Price
		Total	

Server

Warm welcome? _____

Attentiveness and pace of service _____

Gave good recommendations? _____

Accuracy of service _____

Beverage Service

Good recommendations? _____   Checked ID? _____

Experience? _____   Quality of drinks _____

Restaurant

Restaurant cleanliness _____

Restroom cleanliness _____

Overall Impressions

Would you recommend this restaurant? _____

Opportunities for improvement _____

Mileage _____   Compensation _____   Received _____

Restaurant _____ Date of visit _____ Time _____

Server name _____ Manager on duty _____

Party member	Meal ordered	Quality	Price
		Total	

Server

Warm welcome? _____

Attentiveness and pace of service _____

Gave good recommendations? _____

Accuracy of service _____

Beverage Service

Good recommendations? _____ Checked ID? _____

Experience? _____ Quality of drinks _____

Restaurant

Restaurant cleanliness _____

Restroom cleanliness _____

Overall Impressions

Would you recommend this restaurant? _____

Opportunities for improvement _____

Mileage _____ Compensation _____ Received _____

Restaurant _____ Date of visit _____ Time _____

Server name _____ Manager on duty _____

Party member	Meal ordered	Quality	Price
		Total	

┌─ **Server** ─────────────────────────────┐

Warm welcome? _____

Attentiveness and pace of service _____

Gave good recommendations? _____

Accuracy of service _____

└──┘

┌─ **Beverage Service** ───────────────────┐

Good recommendations? _____ Checked ID? _____

Experience? _____ Quality of drinks _____

└──┘

┌─ **Restaurant** ─────────────────────────┐

Restaurant cleanliness _____

Restroom cleanliness _____

└──┘

┌─ **Overall Impressions** ────────────────┐

Would you recommend this restaurant? _____

Opportunities for improvement _____

└──┘

Mileage _____ Compensation _____ Received _____

Restaurant _____ Date of visit _____ Time _____

Server name _____ Manager on duty _____

Party member	Meal ordered	Quality	Price
		Total	

Server

Warm welcome? _____

Attentiveness and pace of service _____

Gave good recommendations? _____

Accuracy of service _____

Beverage Service

Good recommendations? _____   Checked ID? _____

Experience? _____   Quality of drinks _____

Restaurant

Restaurant cleanliness _____

Restroom cleanliness _____

Overall Impressions

Would you recommend this restaurant? _____

Opportunities for improvement _____

Mileage _____   Compensation _____   Received _____

Restaurant _____   Date of visit _____   Time _____

Server name _____   Manager on duty _____

Party member	Meal ordered	Quality	Price
		Total	

Server

Warm welcome? _____

Attentiveness and pace of service _____

Gave good recommendations? _____

Accuracy of service _____

Beverage Service

Good recommendations? _____   Checked ID? _____

Experience? _____   Quality of drinks _____

Restaurant

Restaurant cleanliness _____

Restroom cleanliness _____

Overall Impressions

Would you recommend this restaurant? _____

Opportunities for improvement _____

Mileage _____   Compensation _____   Received _____

Restarant _____   Date of visit _____   Time _____

Server name _____   Manager on duty _____

Party member	Meal ordered	Quality	Price
		Total	

Server

Warm welcome? _____

Attentiveness and pace of service _____

Gave good recommendations? _____

Accuracy of service _____

Beverage Service

Good recommendations? _____   Checked ID? _____

Experience? _____   Quality of drinks _____

Restaurant

Restaurant cleanliness _____

Restroom cleanliness _____

Overall Impressions

Would you recommend this restaurant? _____

Opportunities for improvement _____

Mileage _____   Compensation _____   Received _____

Restaurant _____ Date of visit _____ Time _____

Server name _____ Manager on duty _____

Party member	Meal ordered	Quality	Price
		Total	

Server

Warm welcome? _____

Attentiveness and pace of service _____

Gave good recommendations? _____

Accuracy of service _____

Beverage Service

Good recommendations? _____ Checked ID? _____

Experience? _____ Quality of drinks _____

Restaurant

Restaurant cleanliness _____

Restroom cleanliness _____

Overall Impressions

Would you recommend this restaurant? _____

Opportunities for improvement _____

Mileage _____ Compensation _____ Received _____

Restaurant _____ Date of visit _____ Time _____

Server name _____ Manager on duty _____

Party member	Meal ordered	Quality	Price
	Total		

Server

Warm welcome? _____

Attentiveness and pace of service _____

Gave good recommendations? _____

Accuracy of service _____

Beverage Service

Good recommendations? _____ Checked ID? _____

Experience? _____ Quality of drinks _____

Restaurant

Restaurant cleanliness _____

Restroom cleanliness _____

Overall Impressions

Would you recommend this restaurant? _____

Opportunities for improvement _____

Mileage _____ Compensation _____ Received _____

| Restaurant | _____ | Date of visit _____ | Time _____ |

Server name _____   Manager on duty _____

Party member	Meal ordered	Quality	Price
		Total	

Server

Warm welcome? _____

Attentiveness and pace of service _____

Gave good recommendations? _____

Accuracy of service _____

Beverage Service

Good recommendations? _____   Checked ID? _____

Experience? _____   Quality of drinks _____

Restaurant

Restaurant cleanliness _____

Restroom cleanliness _____

Overall Impressions

Would you recommend this restaurant? _____

Opportunities for improvement _____

Mileage _____   Compensation _____   Received _____

Restaurant _____ Date of visit _____ Time _____

Server name _____ Manager on duty _____

Party member	Meal ordered	Quality	Price
		Total	

<table>
<tr><td colspan="2">

Server
</td></tr>
</table>

Server

Warm welcome? _____

Attentiveness and pace of service _____

Gave good recommendations? _____

Accuracy of service _____

Beverage Service

Good recommendations? _____ Checked ID? _____

Experience? _____ Quality of drinks _____

Restaurant

Restaurant cleanliness _____

Restroom cleanliness _____

Overall Impressions

Would you recommend this restaurant? _____

Opportunities for improvement _____

Mileage _____ Compensation _____ Received _____

Restaurant _____ Date of visit _____ Time _____

Server name _____ Manager on duty _____

Party member	Meal ordered	Quality	Price
		Total	

┌─ **Server** ──────────────────────────
│ Warm welcome? _____
│ Attentiveness and pace of service _____
│ Gave good recommendations? _____
│ Accuracy of service _____
└──────────────────────────

┌─ **Beverage Service** ──────────────────
│ Good recommendations? _____ Checked ID? _____
│ Experience? _____ Quality of drinks _____
└──────────────────────────

┌─ **Restaurant** ──────────────────────
│ Restaurant cleanliness _____
│ Restroom cleanliness _____
└──────────────────────────

┌─ **Overall Impressions** ────────────────
│ Would you recommend this restaurant? _____
│ Opportunities for improvement _____
└──────────────────────────

Mileage _____ Compensation _____ Received _____

Restaurant _____ Date of visit _____ Time _____

Server name _____ Manager on duty _____

Party member	Meal ordered	Quality	Price
	Total		

Server

Warm welcome? _____

Attentiveness and pace of service _____

Gave good recommendations? _____

Accuracy of service _____

Beverage Service

Good recommendations? _____ Checked ID? _____

Experience? _____ Quality of drinks _____

Restaurant

Restaurant cleanliness _____

Restroom cleanliness _____

Overall Impressions

Would you recommend this restaurant? _____

Opportunities for improvement _____

Mileage _____ Compensation _____ Received _____

Restaurant _____ Date of visit _____ Time _____

Server name _____ Manager on duty _____

Party member	Meal ordered	Quality	Price
		Total	

Server

Warm welcome? _____

Attentiveness and pace of service _____

Gave good recommendations? _____

Accuracy of service _____

Beverage Service

Good recommendations? _____ Checked ID? _____

Experience? _____ Quality of drinks _____

Restaurant

Restaurant cleanliness _____

Restroom cleanliness _____

Overall Impressions

Would you recommend this restaurant? _____

Opportunities for improvement _____

Mileage _____ Compensation _____ Received _____

Restaurant _____   Date of visit _____   Time _____

Server name _____   Manager on duty _____

Party member	Meal ordered	Quality	Price
		Total	

Server

Warm welcome? _____

Attentiveness and pace of service _____

Gave good recommendations? _____

Accuracy of service _____

Beverage Service

Good recommendations? _____   Checked ID? _____

Experience? _____   Quality of drinks _____

Restaurant

Restaurant cleanliness _____

Restroom cleanliness _____

Overall Impressions

Would you recommend this restaurant? _____

Opportunities for improvement _____

Mileage _____   Compensation _____   Received _____

Restaurant _____ Date of visit _____ Time _____

Server name _____ Manager on duty _____

Party member	Meal ordered	Quality	Price
		Total	

Server

Warm welcome? _____

Attentiveness and pace of service _____

Gave good recommendations? _____

Accuracy of service _____

Beverage Service

Good recommendations? _____ Checked ID? _____

Experience? _____ Quality of drinks _____

Restaurant

Restaurant cleanliness _____

Restroom cleanliness _____

Overall Impressions

Would you recommend this restaurant? _____

Opportunities for improvement _____

Mileage _____ Compensation _____ Received _____

Restaurant _____ Date of visit _____ Time _____

Server name _____ Manager on duty _____

Party member	Meal ordered	Quality	Price
		Total	

Server

Warm welcome? _____

Attentiveness and pace of service _____

Gave good recommendations? _____

Accuracy of service _____

Beverage Service

Good recommendations? _____   Checked ID? _____

Experience? _____   Quality of drinks _____

Restaurant

Restaurant cleanliness _____

Restroom cleanliness _____

Overall Impressions

Would you recommend this restaurant? _____

Opportunities for improvement _____

Mileage _____   Compensation _____   Received _____

Restaurant _____ Date of visit _____ Time _____

Server name _____ Manager on duty _____

Party member	Meal ordered	Quality	Price
		Total	

Server

Warm welcome? _____

Attentiveness and pace of service _____

Gave good recommendations? _____

Accuracy of service _____

Beverage Service

Good recommendations? _____ Checked ID? _____

Experience? _____ Quality of drinks _____

Restaurant

Restaurant cleanliness _____

Restroom cleanliness _____

Overall Impressions

Would you recommend this restaurant? _____

Opportunities for improvement _____

Mileage _____ Compensation _____ Received _____

| Restaurant _____ | Date of visit _____ | Time _____ |

Server name _____   Manager on duty _____

Party member	Meal ordered	Quality	Price
		Total	

Server

Warm welcome? _____

Attentiveness and pace of service _____

Gave good recommendations? _____

Accuracy of service _____

Beverage Service

Good recommendations? _____   Checked ID? _____

Experience? _____   Quality of drinks _____

Restaurant

Restaurant cleanliness _____

Restroom cleanliness _____

Overall Impressions

Would you recommend this restaurant? _____

Opportunities for improvement _____

Mileage _____   Compensation _____   Received _____

| Restaurant | | Date of visit | | Time | |

Server name _____   Manager on duty _____

Party member	Meal ordered	Quality	Price
		Total	

Server

Warm welcome? _____

Attentiveness and pace of service _____

Gave good recommendations? _____

Accuracy of service _____

Beverage Service

Good recommendations? _____   Checked ID? _____

Experience? _____   Quality of drinks _____

Restaurant

Restaurant cleanliness _____

Restroom cleanliness _____

Overall Impressions

Would you recommend this restaurant? _____

Opportunities for improvement _____

Mileage _____   Compensation _____   Received _____

Restaurant _____ Date of visit _____ Time _____

Server name _____ Manager on duty _____

Party member	Meal ordered	Quality	Price
		Total	

Server

Warm welcome? _____

Attentiveness and pace of service _____

Gave good recommendations? _____

Accuracy of service _____

Beverage Service

Good recommendations? _____   Checked ID? _____

Experience? _____   Quality of drinks _____

Restaurant

Restaurant cleanliness _____

Restroom cleanliness _____

Overall Impressions

Would you recommend this restaurant? _____

Opportunities for improvement _____

Mileage _____   Compensation _____   Received _____

| Restaurant | _____ | Date of visit | _____ | Time | _____ |

Restaurant _____   Date of visit _____   Time _____

Server name _____   Manager on duty _____

Party member	Meal ordered	Quality	Price
		Total	

Server

Warm welcome? _____

Attentiveness and pace of service _____

Gave good recommendations? _____

Accuracy of service _____

Beverage Service

Good recommendations? _____   Checked ID? _____

Experience? _____   Quality of drinks _____

Restaurant

Restaurant cleanliness _____

Restroom cleanliness _____

Overall Impressions

Would you recommend this restaurant? _____

Opportunities for improvement _____

Mileage _____   Compensation _____   Received _____

Restaurant _____ Date of visit _____ Time _____

Server name _____ Manager on duty _____

Party member	Meal ordered	Quality	Price
		Total	

Server

Warm welcome? _____

Attentiveness and pace of service _____

Gave good recommendations? _____

Accuracy of service _____

Beverage Service

Good recommendations? _____ Checked ID? _____

Experience? _____ Quality of drinks _____

Restaurant

Restaurant cleanliness _____

Restroom cleanliness _____

Overall Impressions

Would you recommend this restaurant? _____

Opportunities for improvement _____

Mileage _____ Compensation _____ Received _____

Restaurant _____ Date of visit _____ Time _____

Server name _____ Manager on duty _____

Party member	Meal ordered	Quality	Price
		Total	

Server

Warm welcome? _____

Attentiveness and pace of service _____

Gave good recommendations? _____

Accuracy of service _____

Beverage Service

Good recommendations? _____   Checked ID? _____

Experience? _____   Quality of drinks _____

Restaurant

Restaurant cleanliness _____

Restroom cleanliness _____

Overall Impressions

Would you recommend this restaurant? _____

Opportunities for improvement _____

Mileage _____   Compensation _____   Received _____

Restaurant _____ Date of visit _____ Time _____

Server name _____ Manager on duty _____

Party member	Meal ordered	Quality	Price
		Total	

┌─ **Server** ─────────────────────────────────┐

　　　　　　　Warm welcome? _____

Attentiveness and pace of service _____

　　Gave good recommendations? _____

　　　　　Accuracy of service _____

└──────────────────────────────────────┘

┌─ **Beverage Service** ───────────────────────┐

Good recommendations? _____ Checked ID? _____

　　　Experience? _____ Quality of drinks _____

└──────────────────────────────────────┘

┌─ **Restaurant** ─────────────────────────────┐

Restaurant cleanliness _____

Restroom cleanliness _____

└──────────────────────────────────────┘

┌─ **Overall Impressions** ────────────────────┐

Would you recommend this restaurant? _____

　　Opportunities for improvement _____

└──────────────────────────────────────┘

Mileage _____ Compensation _____ Received _____

Restaurant _____ Date of visit _____ Time _____

Server name _____ Manager on duty _____

Party member	Meal ordered	Quality	Price
		Total	

Server

Warm welcome? _____

Attentiveness and pace of service _____

Gave good recommendations? _____

Accuracy of service _____

Beverage Service

Good recommendations? _____ Checked ID? _____

Experience? _____ Quality of drinks _____

Restaurant

Restaurant cleanliness _____

Restroom cleanliness _____

Overall Impressions

Would you recommend this restaurant? _____

Opportunities for improvement _____

Mileage _____ Compensation _____ Received _____

Restaurant _____ Date of visit _____ Time _____

Server name _____ Manager on duty _____

Party member	Meal ordered	Quality	Price
		Total	

Server

Warm welcome? _____

Attentiveness and pace of service _____

Gave good recommendations? _____

Accuracy of service _____

Beverage Service

Good recommendations? _____ Checked ID? _____

Experience? _____ Quality of drinks _____

Restaurant

Restaurant cleanliness _____

Restroom cleanliness _____

Overall Impressions

Would you recommend this restaurant? _____

Opportunities for improvement _____

Mileage _____ Compensation _____ Received _____

Restaurant _____ Date of visit _____ Time _____

Server name _____ Manager on duty _____

Party member	Meal ordered	Quality	Price
		Total	

Server

Warm welcome? _____

Attentiveness and pace of service _____

Gave good recommendations? _____

Accuracy of service _____

Beverage Service

Good recommendations? _____ Checked ID? _____

Experience? _____ Quality of drinks _____

Restaurant

Restaurant cleanliness _____

Restroom cleanliness _____

Overall Impressions

Would you recommend this restaurant? _____

Opportunities for improvement _____

Mileage _____ Compensation _____ Received _____

Restaurant _____ Date of visit _____ Time _____

Server name _____ Manager on duty _____

Party member	Meal ordered	Quality	Price
	Total		

Server

Warm welcome? _____

Attentiveness and pace of service _____

Gave good recommendations? _____

Accuracy of service _____

Beverage Service

Good recommendations? _____   Checked ID? _____

Experience? _____   Quality of drinks _____

Restaurant

Restaurant cleanliness _____

Restroom cleanliness _____

Overall Impressions

Would you recommend this restaurant? _____

Opportunities for improvement _____

Mileage _____   Compensation _____   Received _____

Restaurant _____ Date of visit _____ Time _____

Server name _____ Manager on duty _____

Party member	Meal ordered	Quality	Price
		Total	

Server

Warm welcome? _____

Attentiveness and pace of service _____

Gave good recommendations? _____

Accuracy of service _____

Beverage Service

Good recommendations? _____ Checked ID? _____

Experience? _____ Quality of drinks _____

Restaurant

Restaurant cleanliness _____

Restroom cleanliness _____

Overall Impressions

Would you recommend this restaurant? _____

Opportunities for improvement _____

Mileage _____ Compensation _____ Received _____

Restaurant _____ Date of visit _____ Time _____

Server name _____ Manager on duty _____

Party member	Meal ordered	Quality	Price
	Total		

Server

Warm welcome? _____

Attentiveness and pace of service _____

Gave good recommendations? _____

Accuracy of service _____

Beverage Service

Good recommendations? _____   Checked ID? _____

Experience? _____   Quality of drinks _____

Restaurant

Restaurant cleanliness _____

Restroom cleanliness _____

Overall Impressions

Would you recommend this restaurant? _____

Opportunities for improvement _____

Mileage _____   Compensation _____   Received _____

| Restaurant | | Date of visit | | Time | |

Server name _____ Manager on duty _____

Party member	Meal ordered	Quality	Price
		Total	

Server

Warm welcome? _____

Attentiveness and pace of service _____

Gave good recommendations? _____

Accuracy of service _____

Beverage Service

Good recommendations? _____   Checked ID? _____

Experience? _____   Quality of drinks _____

Restaurant

Restaurant cleanliness _____

Restroom cleanliness _____

Overall Impressions

Would you recommend this restaurant? _____

Opportunities for improvement _____

Mileage _____ Compensation _____ Received _____

Restaurant _____ Date of visit _____ Time _____

Server name _____ Manager on duty _____

Party member	Meal ordered	Quality	Price
		Total	

Server

Warm welcome? _____

Attentiveness and pace of service _____

Gave good recommendations? _____

Accuracy of service _____

Beverage Service

Good recommendations? _____ Checked ID? _____

Experience? _____ Quality of drinks _____

Restaurant

Restaurant cleanliness _____

Restroom cleanliness _____

Overall Impressions

Would you recommend this restaurant? _____

Opportunities for improvement _____

Mileage _____ Compensation _____ Received _____

| Restaurant | _____ | Date of visit | _____ | Time | _____ |

Server name _____ Manager on duty _____

Party member	Meal ordered	Quality	Price
		Total	

Server

Warm welcome?	_____
Attentiveness and pace of service	_____
Gave good recommendations?	_____
Accuracy of service	_____

Beverage Service

Good recommendations?	_____	Checked ID?	_____
Experience?	_____	Quality of drinks	_____

Restaurant

Restaurant cleanliness	_____
Restroom cleanliness	_____

Overall Impressions

Would you recommend this restaurant?	_____
Opportunities for improvement	_____

Mileage _____ Compensation _____ Received _____

Restaurant _____   Date of visit _____   Time _____

Server name _____   Manager on duty _____

Party member	Meal ordered	Quality	Price
		Total	

Server

Warm welcome? _____

Attentiveness and pace of service _____

Gave good recommendations? _____

Accuracy of service _____

Beverage Service

Good recommendations? _____   Checked ID? _____

Experience? _____   Quality of drinks _____

Restaurant

Restaurant cleanliness _____

Restroom cleanliness _____

Overall Impressions

Would you recommend this restaurant? _____

Opportunities for improvement _____

Mileage _____   Compensation _____   Received _____

Restaurant _____ Date of visit _____ Time _____

Server name _____ Manager on duty _____

Party member	Meal ordered	Quality	Price
		Total	

Server

Warm welcome? _____

Attentiveness and pace of service _____

Gave good recommendations? _____

Accuracy of service _____

Beverage Service

Good recommendations? _____ Checked ID? _____

Experience? _____ Quality of drinks _____

Restaurant

Restaurant cleanliness _____

Restroom cleanliness _____

Overall Impressions

Would you recommend this restaurant? _____

Opportunities for improvement _____

Mileage _____ Compensation _____ Received _____

Restaurant _____ Date of visit _____ Time _____

Server name _____ Manager on duty _____

Party member	Meal ordered	Quality	Price
		Total	

Server

Warm welcome? _____

Attentiveness and pace of service _____

Gave good recommendations? _____

Accuracy of service _____

Beverage Service

Good recommendations? _____   Checked ID? _____

Experience? _____   Quality of drinks _____

Restaurant

Restaurant cleanliness _____

Restroom cleanliness _____

Overall Impressions

Would you recommend this restaurant? _____

Opportunities for improvement _____

Mileage _____ Compensation _____ Received _____

Restaurant _____ Date of visit _____ Time _____

Server name _____ Manager on duty _____

Party member	Meal ordered	Quality	Price
		Total	

Server

Warm welcome? _____

Attentiveness and pace of service _____

Gave good recommendations? _____

Accuracy of service _____

Beverage Service

Good recommendations? _____ Checked ID? _____

Experience? _____ Quality of drinks _____

Restaurant

Restaurant cleanliness _____

Restroom cleanliness _____

Overall Impressions

Would you recommend this restaurant? _____

Opportunities for improvement _____

Mileage _____ Compensation _____ Received _____

Restaurant _____ Date of visit _____ Time _____

Server name _____ Manager on duty _____

Party member	Meal ordered	Quality	Price
		Total	

Server

Warm welcome? _____

Attentiveness and pace of service _____

Gave good recommendations? _____

Accuracy of service _____

Beverage Service

Good recommendations? _____ Checked ID? _____

Experience? _____ Quality of drinks _____

Restaurant

Restaurant cleanliness _____

Restroom cleanliness _____

Overall Impressions

Would you recommend this restaurant? _____

Opportunities for improvement _____

Mileage _____ Compensation _____ Received _____

Restaurant _____ Date of visit _____ Time _____

Server name _____ Manager on duty _____

Party member	Meal ordered	Quality	Price
		Total	

Server

Warm welcome? _____

Attentiveness and pace of service _____

Gave good recommendations? _____

Accuracy of service _____

Beverage Service

Good recommendations? _____ Checked ID? _____

Experience? _____ Quality of drinks _____

Restaurant

Restaurant cleanliness _____

Restroom cleanliness _____

Overall Impressions

Would you recommend this restaurant? _____

Opportunities for improvement _____

Mileage _____ Compensation _____ Received _____

Restaurant _____ Date of visit _____ Time _____

Server name _____ Manager on duty _____

Party member	Meal ordered	Quality	Price
	Total		

Server

Warm welcome? _____

Attentiveness and pace of service _____

Gave good recommendations? _____

Accuracy of service _____

Beverage Service

Good recommendations? _____ Checked ID? _____

Experience? _____ Quality of drinks _____

Restaurant

Restaurant cleanliness _____

Restroom cleanliness _____

Overall Impressions

Would you recommend this restaurant? _____

Opportunities for improvement _____

Mileage _____ Compensation _____ Received _____

| Restaurant | _____ | Date of visit _____ | Time _____ |

Server name _____   Manager on duty _____

Party member	Meal ordered	Quality	Price
		Total	

Server

Warm welcome? _____

Attentiveness and pace of service _____

Gave good recommendations? _____

Accuracy of service _____

Beverage Service

Good recommendations? _____   Checked ID? _____

Experience? _____   Quality of drinks _____

Restaurant

Restaurant cleanliness _____

Restroom cleanliness _____

Overall Impressions

Would you recommend this restaurant? _____

Opportunities for improvement _____

Mileage _____   Compensation _____   Received _____

Restaurant _____ Date of visit _____ Time _____

Server name _____ Manager on duty _____

Party member	Meal ordered	Quality	Price
		Total	

Server

Warm welcome? _____

Attentiveness and pace of service _____

Gave good recommendations? _____

Accuracy of service _____

Beverage Service

Good recommendations? _____ Checked ID? _____

Experience? _____ Quality of drinks _____

Restaurant

Restaurant cleanliness _____

Restroom cleanliness _____

Overall Impressions

Would you recommend this restaurant? _____

Opportunities for improvement _____

Mileage _____ Compensation _____ Received _____

| Restaurant | _____ | Date of visit | _____ | Time | _____ |

| Server name | _____ | Manager on duty | _____ |

Party member	Meal ordered	Quality	Price
		Total	

Server

Warm welcome? _____

Attentiveness and pace of service _____

Gave good recommendations? _____

Accuracy of service _____

Beverage Service

Good recommendations? _____   Checked ID? _____

Experience? _____   Quality of drinks _____

Restaurant

Restaurant cleanliness _____

Restroom cleanliness _____

Overall Impressions

Would you recommend this restaurant? _____

Opportunities for improvement _____

Mileage _____   Compensation _____   Received _____

Restaurant _____ Date of visit _____ Time _____

Server name _____ Manager on duty _____

Party member	Meal ordered	Quality	Price
		Total	

┌─ **Server** ─────────────────────────────
│
│   Warm welcome? _____
│
│ Attentiveness and pace of service _____
│
│   Gave good recommendations? _____
│
│   Accuracy of service _____
│

┌─ **Beverage Service** ─────────────────────
│
│ Good recommendations? _____   Checked ID? _____
│
│   Experience? _____   Quality of drinks _____
│

┌─ **Restaurant** ───────────────────────────
│
│ Restaurant cleanliness _____
│
│ Restroom cleanliness _____
│

┌─ **Overall Impressions** ──────────────────
│
│ Would you recommend this restaurant? _____
│
│   Opportunities for improvement _____
│

Mileage _____ Compensation _____ Received _____

Restaurant _____ Date of visit _____ Time _____

Server name _____ Manager on duty _____

Party member	Meal ordered	Quality	Price
		Total	

Server

Warm welcome? _____

Attentiveness and pace of service _____

Gave good recommendations? _____

Accuracy of service _____

Beverage Service

Good recommendations? _____ Checked ID? _____

Experience? _____ Quality of drinks _____

Restaurant

Restaurant cleanliness _____

Restroom cleanliness _____

Overall Impressions

Would you recommend this restaurant? _____

Opportunities for improvement _____

Mileage _____ Compensation _____ Received _____

Restaurant _____ Date of visit _____ Time _____

Server name _____ Manager on duty _____

Party member	Meal ordered	Quality	Price
		Total	

Server

Warm welcome? _____

Attentiveness and pace of service _____

Gave good recommendations? _____

Accuracy of service _____

Beverage Service

Good recommendations? _____ Checked ID? _____

Experience? _____ Quality of drinks _____

Restaurant

Restaurant cleanliness _____

Restroom cleanliness _____

Overall Impressions

Would you recommend this restaurant? _____

Opportunities for improvement _____

Mileage _____ Compensation _____ Received _____

Restaurant _____ Date of visit _____ Time _____

Server name _____ Manager on duty _____

Party member	Meal ordered	Quality	Price
		Total	

Server

Warm welcome? _____

Attentiveness and pace of service _____

Gave good recommendations? _____

Accuracy of service _____

Beverage Service

Good recommendations? _____   Checked ID? _____

Experience? _____   Quality of drinks _____

Restaurant

Restaurant cleanliness _____

Restroom cleanliness _____

Overall Impressions

Would you recommend this restaurant? _____

Opportunities for improvement _____

Mileage _____   Compensation _____   Received _____

Restaurant _____ Date of visit _____ Time _____

Server name _____ Manager on duty _____

Party member	Meal ordered	Quality	Price
		Total	

Server

Warm welcome? _____

Attentiveness and pace of service _____

Gave good recommendations? _____

Accuracy of service _____

Beverage Service

Good recommendations? _____ Checked ID? _____

Experience? _____ Quality of drinks _____

Restaurant

Restaurant cleanliness _____

Restroom cleanliness _____

Overall Impressions

Would you recommend this restaurant? _____

Opportunities for improvement _____

Mileage _____ Compensation _____ Received _____

| Restaurant | | Date of visit | | Time | |

Server name _____   Manager on duty _____

Party member	Meal ordered	Quality	Price
		Total	

Server

Warm welcome? _____

Attentiveness and pace of service _____

Gave good recommendations? _____

Accuracy of service _____

Beverage Service

Good recommendations? _____   Checked ID? _____

Experience? _____   Quality of drinks _____

Restaurant

Restaurant cleanliness _____

Restroom cleanliness _____

Overall Impressions

Would you recommend this restaurant? _____

Opportunities for improvement _____

Mileage _____   Compensation _____   Received _____